Sharing Joy in the Neighborhood

by Alexandra Cassel Schwartz
poses and layouts by Jason Fruchter

Simon Spotlight

New York London Toronto Sydney New Delhi

SIMON SPOTLIGHT
An imprint of Simon & Schuster Children's Publishing Division
1230 Avenue of the Americas, New York, New York 10020
This Simon Spotlight paperback edition May 2022
© 2022 The Fred Rogers Company.
All rights reserved, including the right of reproduction in whole or in part in any form.
SIMON SPOTLIGHT and colophon are registered trademarks of Simon & Schuster, Inc.
For information about special discounts for bulk purchases, please contact Simon & Schuster
Special Sales at 1-866-506-1949 or business@simonandschuster.com.
Manufactured in the United States of America 0922 LAK
10 9 8 7 6 5 4 3 2
ISBN 978-1-6659-1285-3
ISBN 978-1-6659-1286-0 (ebook)

It was a quiet day in the neighborhood outside the bungalow where Daniel stood. "Hi, neighbor!" he said as he pointed ahead. "Look! Do you see what I see?" Daniel said.

Right away, Daniel and his dad checked the mail.
"Awww!" Dad Tiger said with a long exhale.
There was a tigertastic letter inside.
"It's from my Grandpere!" Daniel said with pride.

Receiving this letter gave Daniel such joy.
"This gift is much better than any toy!"
Daniel said, "Seeing how this made me feel good,
I want to share joy with the WHOLE neighborhood!"

Dad thought that idea was grr-ific indeed.
They'd have Mr. McFeely send letters with speed!

So Daniel worked hard with crayons and paper. He wanted to send joy to every neighbor!

First, Daniel drew pictures for each of his friends. "I love all the time we spend playing pretend!"

One for Katerina, Prince Wednesday, and O.
Daniel said, "And here's what I want them to know. . . .
Even though we're not always together each day,
I'm always thinking about the times that we play!"

Daniel sent more pictures. He was quite busy!
One for Miss Elaina, Jodi, and Chrissie.
"I want to make each of them feel happy too!"
Then the neighborhood joy grew and grew and grew.

Daniel wrote a letter to his teacher next. "Thank you for always helping me do my best."

The whole neighborhood felt Daniel's joy right away.
He turned around what was an ordinary day.
But there was one person Daniel could not leave out.
"Grandpere! He started what this whole thing's about!"

Grandpere sent joy, and Daniel passed it along.
"And YOU can share joy with a drawing or song!
Oh, but wait!" Daniel Tiger said. "I'm not through!"
"Here's even more joy. . . . Ugga Mugga to you!"

Carefully remove the cards from this book. Draw or write a message to spread joy to your loved ones!